DISNEY · PIXAR

Cars TOON

MATER'S TALL TALES

Adapted by Frank Berrios

CONTENTS

Random House 🏠 New York

Copyright © 2009 Disney Enterprises, Inc./Pixar. Disney/Pixar elements © Disney/Pixar, not including underlying vehicles owned by third parties. Volkswagen trademarks, design patents and copyrights are used with the approval of the owner, Volkswagen AG; Fiat is a trademark of Fiat S.p.A.; Chevrolet Impala is a trademark of General Motors; Mazda Miata is a registered trademark of Mazda Motor Corporation; Pontiac GTO is a trademark of General Motors; Jeep is a registered trademark of DaimlerChrysler; Ferrari elements are trademarks of Ferrari S.p.A.; Sarge's rank insignia design used with the approval of the U.S. Army. Inspired by the Cadillac Ranch by Ant Farm (Lord, Michels and Marquez) © 1974. All rights reserved. Published in the United States by Random House Children's Books, a division of Random House, Inc., 1745 Broadway, New York, NY 10019, and in Canada by Random House of Canada Limited, Toronto, in conjunction with Disney Enterprises, Inc. Random House and the colophon are registered trademarks of Random House, Inc.

ISBN: 978-0-7364-2638-1
www.randomhouse.com/kids
MANUFACTURED IN SINGAPORE
10 9 8 7 6 5

RESCUE SQUAD

MATER

Lightning McQueen and Mater were enjoying a cruise down Main Street when Mater said, "Ya know, I used to be a fire truck."

"What?" said Lightning. He couldn't believe what he was hearing.

"Dadgum right," replied Mater as he started to tell Lightning the story. . . .

4

Mater jumped when he heard the alarm.

"All units, please respond—fire in progress!" blared the voice from the speaker in the fire station.

"That's the old Gasoline and Match Factory!" Mater exclaimed when he heard the address. He was ready!

Mater set off toward the blaze—there was no time to spare.
"Mater One en route," he replied, racing over a hill.

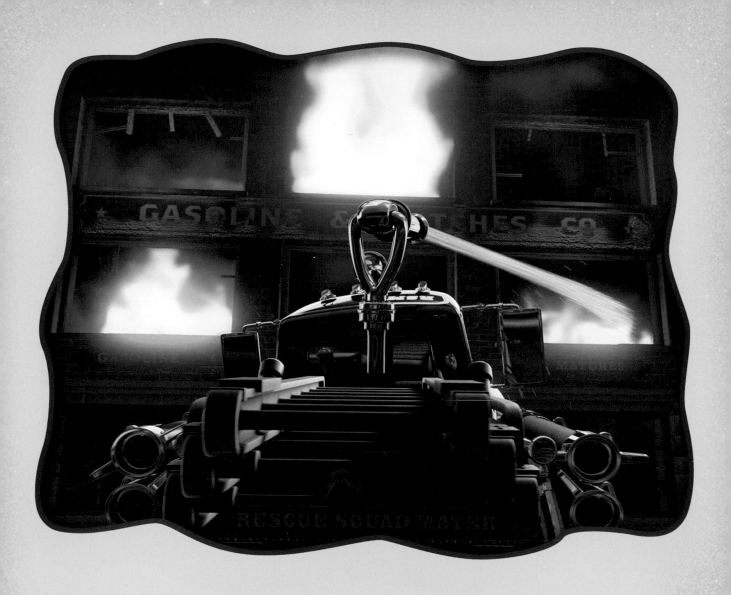

Mater arrived at the scene of the fire and got to work. He used his hose to blast water directly into the burning building.

"Be advised, this is an explosive situation," warned the dispatcher. "Rescue Squad Mater, we're counting on you!"

"Ten-four. I'm on it," replied Mater, shooting more water onto the blaze.

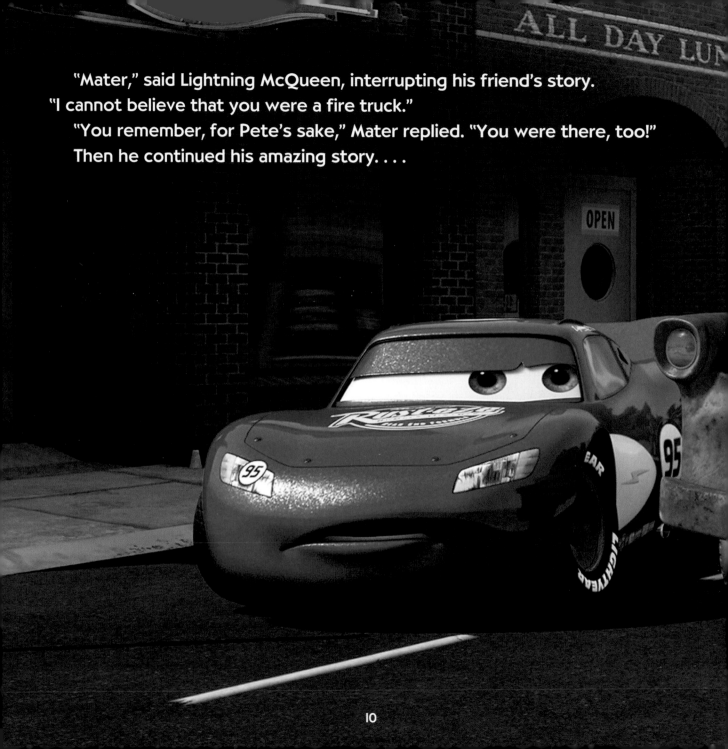

"Mater," said Lightning McQueen, interrupting his friend's story. "I cannot believe that you were a fire truck."

"You remember, for Pete's sake," Mater replied. "You were there, too!"

Then he continued his amazing story. . . .

"Ahhh! Help! Help!" cried Lightning, looking for a way out of the burning building.

"Remain calm," said Mater, soaking his friend with cold water.

Mater quickly spun around and raised his ladder to help Lightning get away from the flames.

"I gotcha," said Mater as he pulled his friend out the window—
just before the building exploded!

Mater rushed Lightning into the back of an ambulance.

"Get him to the hospital! He's overheatin'," said Mater.

The crowd cheered for their hero, Rescue Squad Mater!

"Yay, Mater!" cried Mia.

"Mater's awesome!" added Tia.

Meanwhile, Lightning was being wheeled into the hospital's operating room.

"Huh? What's going on? Where am I?" he asked, confused.

Lightning was shocked when Mater rolled into the room.
"Mater, you're a doctor, too?" Lightning asked.

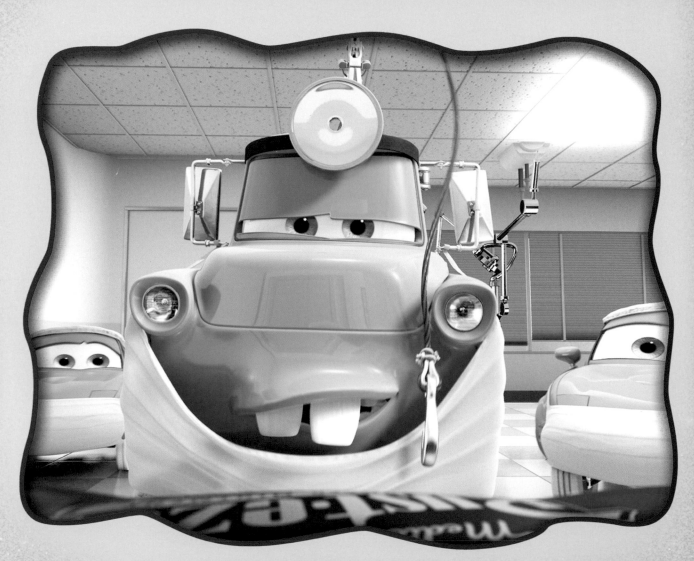

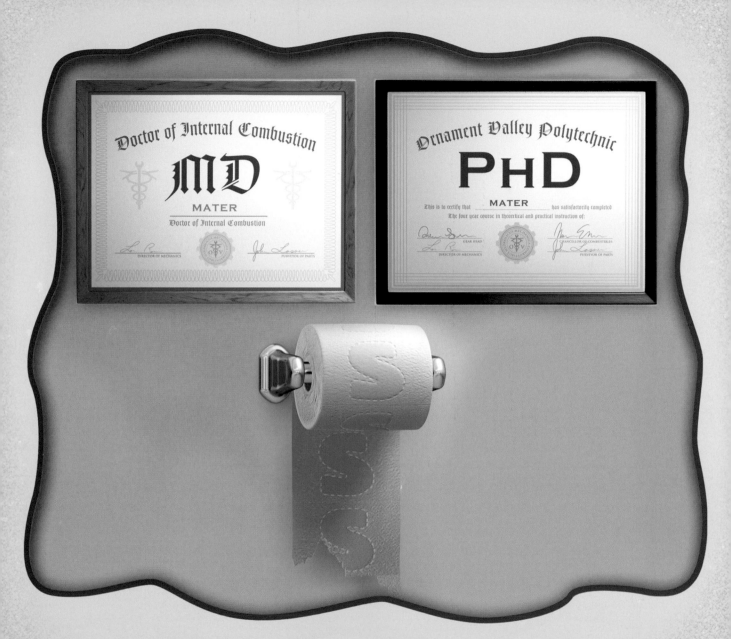

"That's right, buddy," Mater replied. "Got my MD, my PhD, my STP, and my GTO."

"Hey, Doctor," said Nurse GTO as she arrived.

"Everybody stand clear!" Mater warned, preparing to give Lightning's battery a high-voltage charge.

"No, wait—ahhh!" screamed Lightning.

"Well, what happened?" asked Lightning.

"I saved your life," replied Mater.

"Did not," said Lightning.

"Did so," said Mater.

"Not!" replied Lightning.

Just then, Nurse GTO drove by.
"Hello, Doctor," she said to Mater.

"Did so," said Mater, leaving Lightning McQueen speechless.

MATER

THE
GREATER

Lightning McQueen and some friends were enjoying a quiet afternoon at Flo's when they heard the unmistakable sounds of an engine revving up and wheels screeching on pavement.

They looked up just in time to see Mater flying through the air.
Whoosh!

"Whoooaaah!" Mater screamed as he zoomed by and landed on
a pile of oilcans.

"Mater, are you all right?" asked Lightning as he checked on his friend.

"Well, of course I'm all right," replied Mater. "I used to be a daredevil."

"What?" said Lightning.

"That's right," said Mater as he started to tell his story. "Folks would come from all around to see my stunts. . . ."

"Ladies and gentlecars, Mater the Greater!" screamed the announcer when Mater entered the stadium. The crowd went wild!

But Mater wasn't distracted by the crowd—he was focused.
He stared at the line of cars he was about to jump over—and gulped.
It was a **really** long line!

But nothing could stop him now. He revved up his engine and raced toward the ramp.

"And he's off!" yelled the announcer.

Mater hit the ramp going full speed. He gunned his engine for all the power he'd need to make the jump. Then . . . he was airborne!

But not for long. Mater landed with a thud on the first two cars in the line.

"Oww!" said one of the cars.

" 'Scuse me, pardon me, comin' through, sorry about that," Mater said as he gently rolled his way across the cars.

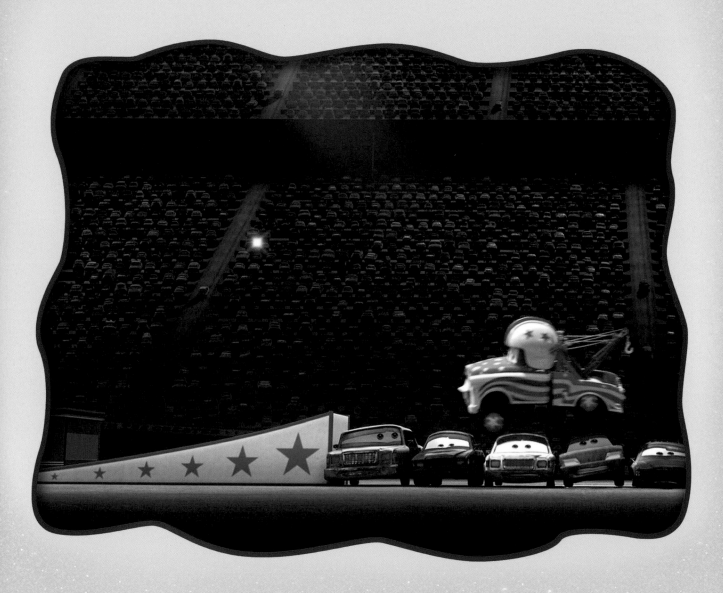

"He did it!" cried the announcer when Mater made it to the other ramp. The crowd cheered! But Mater wasn't done yet.

Next, Mater was shot out of a cannon—and he nearly fried his fenders!

Then he did a high-dive jump!

"Yep, I done busted nearly every part of my body," said Mater, continuing his story. "But the biggest stunt I ever did was jumping Carburetor Canyon."

"You jumped Carburetor Canyon?" asked Lightning. "No way!"

"Yes way," replied Mater. "You remember, you were there, too!"

"Ready, buddy?" asked Mater as he and Lightning sat side by side with rockets strapped to their backs.

Before Lightning could answer, Mater's pitties lit the fuses.

"All right, then, get 'er done!" said Mater as his buddy went blasting down the ramp.

"Ahhhhhhh!" screamed Lightning.

Lightning yelled as he flew into the air over Carburetor Canyon.

But halfway across the canyon, the rockets started to sputter and lose power. . . .

"Well, what happened?" asked Lightning.

"You didn't make it," replied Mater.

Once again, Lightning McQueen was speechless.
"Well, see ya later!" said Mater as he drove away.

EL MATERDOR

Mater and Lightning McQueen were driving down the road when they passed a group of grazing bulldozers.

"Ya know," said Mater, "I used to be a famous bulldozer fighter in Spain."

"They called me El Materdor," Mater declared proudly. . . .

The crowd cheered whenever El Materdor entered the arena.
He was the bravest bulldozer fighter there ever was.

Everybody loved El Materdor—he was fearless! Anyone who looked into his eyes knew that he simply couldn't be defeated.

When the bulldozer entered the arena, a hush came over the crowd.
The bulldozer snarled—and charged El Materdor!

El Materdor waved his red flag. Then he calmly pulled it up at the very last moment, easily dodging the raging machine.

As El Materdor enjoyed the cheers from the crowd, the bulldozer snuck around and charged El Materdor from behind! The bulldozer buried El Materdor in dirt.

The crowd couldn't believe their eyes!

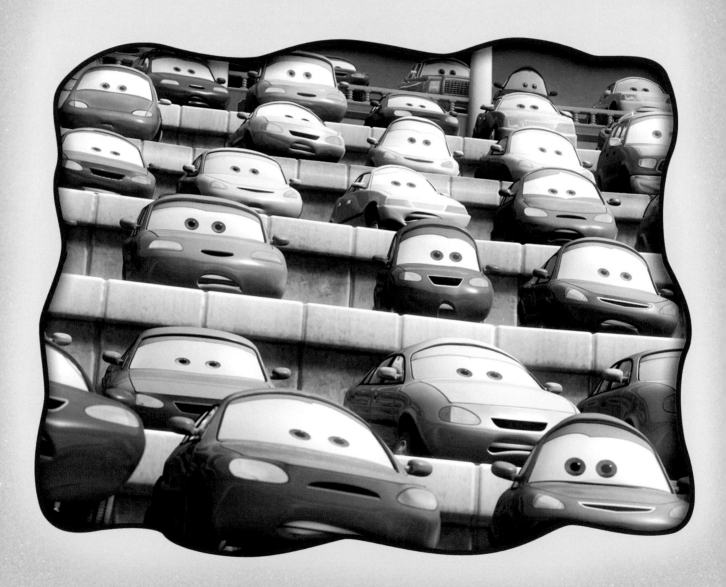

Was this the end for El Materdor?

Suddenly, El Materdor's hook popped out of the dirt, catching the red flag! El Materdor was alive! The crowd cheered!

El Materdor's biggest fans, Señorita Mia and Señorita Tia, were overjoyed to see that their hero had survived.

"Olé!" cried Mia.

"Bravo, Señor Mater!" added Tia.

El Materdor was determined to get back at the bulldozer. He shook off his hood and locked eyes with the big machine. He was ready to rumble!

But now there were **three** bulldozers!

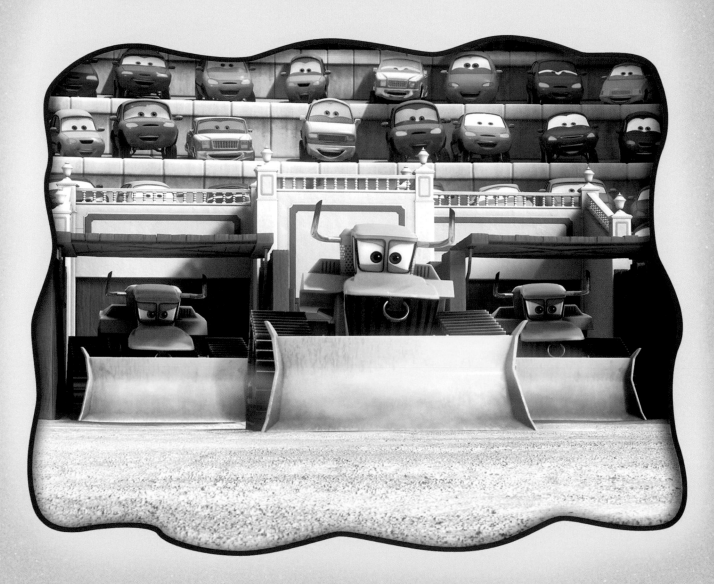

Yikes! Would even the great El Materdor be able to survive against three bulldozers?

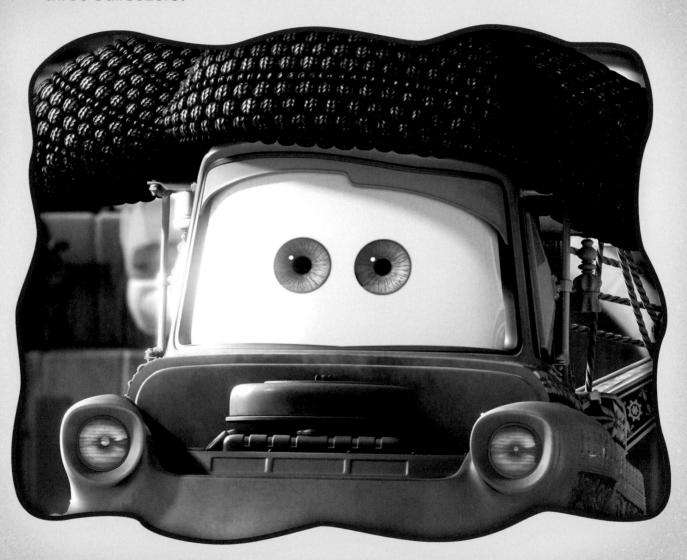

The bulldozers charged El Materdor. But just when they had him surrounded, he leaped into the air! The bulldozers crashed into one another.

"Olé!" said El Materdor, standing proudly atop the defeated bulldozers. "Olé! Bravo, Señor Mater!" cheered the crowd.

But the crowd had cheered too soon!

"There I was, surrounded," Mater said, continuing his story. "Bulldozers all around me . . ."

"What did you do?" asked Lightning McQueen.

"What did I— Well, don't you remember? You were there, too!" replied Mater.

"They sure like your fancy red paint job," Mater told Lightning. "Ahhhhhhhh!" screamed Lightning as the bulldozers chased him all around the arena!

"Mater," said Lightning, "that did **not** happen."

"Well, try telling that to them there bulldozers," said Mater.

"Huh?" asked Lightning. Suddenly, he noticed that they were surrounded by bulldozers.

"Ahhhhhhhhhh!" screamed Lightning as he raced off, with the bulldozers right on his tail.

Just then, two of Mater's biggest fans arrived.

"Señoriters!" said Mater, tossing on his matador hat. "Olé!"

Then the three cars drove off in search of new adventures—
and maybe even a tall tale or two.